2-

FERIDA WOLFF

Seven Loaves of Bread

pictures by KATIE KELLER

Tambourine Books • New York

Library of Congress Cataloging in Publication Data

Wolff, Ferida, 1946—Seven loaves of bread/by Ferida Wolff:
pictures by Katie Keller.—1st ed. p.cm.
Summary: When Milly, who does the baking on the farm, gets sick,
Rose discovers that there are very good reasons for making extra
loaves of bread to share with their animals and friends.
[1. Farm life—Fiction. 2. Baking—Fiction. 3. Bread—Fiction.]
I. Keller, Katie, ill.   II Title.
PZ7.W818554Se1993[E]—dc2092-34313CIPAC
ISBN 0-688-11101-7 (trade)—ISBN 0-688-11112-2 (lib. bdg.)
3 5 7 9 10 8 6 4 2
First edition

For Harriet May Savitz, Mother Hen to us all—F.W.

To Paul—K.K.

Milly and Rose lived on a farm at the top of a hill.

Early each morning when the rooster crowed, Milly went to the kitchen and baked seven loaves of bread.

She gave one loaf to the dog in the yard,

one loaf to the goat in the pen,

one loaf to the hen on her nest,

one loaf to the peddler at the door,

one loaf to the rooster by the fence,

and one loaf to old Mrs. Bandy down the road.

And she gave one loaf to Rose to eat, sliced warm with butter and jam.

"Making seven loaves is too much work," said Rose, who didn't
like to work any harder than she had to.
"It's as easy to make seven as it is to make one," said Milly. "After
all, the dog chases the crows, the goat pulls the cart, the hen gives

us eggs, the peddler brings us supplies, the rooster wakes us up,
and old Mrs. Bandy has stiff hands and cannot make her own.
Come now, Rose, and eat your bread."

One day Milly took sick.

"Rose, you must make the bread," moaned Milly. "And don't forget, seven is as easy as one."

"Now, don't you worry," Rose said. "I'll take care of everything."

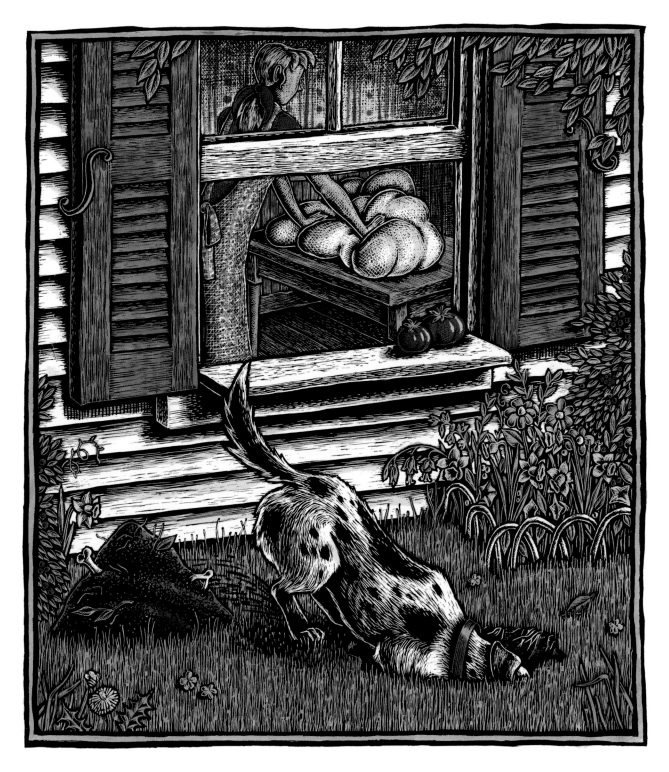

In the kitchen, Rose mixed the dough for the bread.
"That's a lot of dough," she said. "My hands will be tired from kneading."
So Rose, who didn't like to work any harder than she had to, made six
loaves instead of seven. That day the dog did not eat bread. He went
digging for bones and took no notice of the crows.

The next day Milly was no better.

"What Milly needs is a nice pot of mint tea," decided Rose.

But when she went outside to pick some mint, she found crows in the garden and the mint all gone.

"Shoo, shoo, shoo," hollered Rose. It took most of the morning to chase the crows away and Rose, who didn't like to work any harder than she had to, still had to make the bread.

"I'll never have time to make all the bread," Rose said.
So she made only five loaves. When the goat didn't get his bread,
he broke out of his pen to find something else to eat.

The following day Milly was still sick.
"You rest," said Rose. "I'm taking care of everything."

Just then Rose looked out the window and saw the goat nibbling at the laundry on the line.

"What now?" she cried and ran out to chase the goat.

Rose, who didn't like to work any harder than she had to, wondered how she was going to dry all the wet wash with the goat around. "I know," she said. "I'll put the wash in the oven while the bread is baking."

With the laundry in the oven there was only room for four pans. The hen didn't get her bread so she hopped off her nest and went scratching for seed.

Milly was a little better in the morning but still not well enough
to make the bread.

"Some newly laid eggs will help her get stronger," said Rose. She
went out to the barn to gather the eggs but, the nest was empty
and the hen was nowhere to be seen.

"I'll borrow some eggs from Mrs. Bandy," said Rose.
She went to hitch up the cart but the goat was gone. Rose, who
didn't like to work any harder than she had to, walked down the
hill to Mrs. Bandy's farm.

Rose was so tired from her long walk that she made just three
loaves of bread and went to take a nap. When the peddler knocked,
no one answered. He took his sacks of flour down the road.

The next day Milly was even better.
She sat up in bed and called out,
"Rose, are you making the bread?"
But Rose didn't hear Milly. She was
upside down in the flour barrel trying
to reach the flour at the bottom.

"Just look at me," Rose said. She quickly made two loaves and
went off to take a bath.
The rooster scratched around the fence looking for his bread.

At daybreak the rooster was too busy looking for worms to crow. So Rose, who didn't like to work any harder than she had to, slept late. When she awoke, she only had time to make one loaf for Milly before doing her chores. Mrs. Bandy didn't get any bread.

"Are you all better today, Milly?" said Rose.
"Almost," said Milly. "I will rest for one more day and tomorrow I will make the bread."
Good, thought Rose. *At last I won't have to work so hard.*

But when Rose went out to rock on the porch, she groaned.
The farm was a mess. The garden was ruined, the goat was gone,
the hen had stopped laying, and the rooster wouldn't crow. What
would Milly say when she saw the farm?

So instead of rocking, Rose, who didn't like to work any harder than she had to, hoed and replanted the garden.

She chased after the goat,

threw out seed for the rooster
and the hen, and tossed the dog
a meaty bone.

"None of this would have happened
if I had made seven loaves of bread,"
she said. "Milly was right. It's as easy
to make seven as it is to make one—
and a lot less work!"

Rose got up with the sun in the morning. With the last of the flour she mixed and kneaded and shaped the loaves. Before long, the air was filled with the smell of baking bread.

"You're just in time," Rose called to the peddler as he came into the yard with old Mrs. Bandy. "The baking's done. There's bread for everyone!" The rooster fluffed up his feathers and crowed.

The crowing woke Milly. She went to the kitchen to start
the day's baking.

But Rose, who only worked as hard as she had to, said, "Sit down,
Milly. I'm taking care of everything." Then she gave out six loaves
of the warm, sweet bread.

And the seventh she gave to Milly to eat, sliced warm with butter and jam.